For Chez Tom and
Chez Dave

ABOUT THIS BOOK

The illustrations for this book were done in a comfortable chair while listening to records. This book was edited by Andrea Spooner and designed by Bob Shea with art direction from Saho Fujii. The production was supervised by Virginia Lawther, and the production editor was Annie McDonnell. The text was set in Neutraface 2 Text, and the display type is Brothers.

• Little, Brown and Company • Hachette Book Group • 1290 Avenue of the Americas, New York, NY 10104 • Visit us at LBYR.com • First Edition: August 2021 • Little, Brown and Company is a division of Hachette Book Group, Inc. • The Little, Brown name and logo are trademarks of Hachette Book Group, Inc. • The publisher is not responsible for websites (or their content) that are not owned by the publisher. • Library of Congress Cataloging-in-Publication Data • Names: Shea, Bob, author, illustrator. • Title: Chez Bob / Bob Shea. • Description: First edition. | New York : Little, Brown and Company, 2021. | Audience: Ages 4–8. | Summary: "A lazy alligator comes up with a plan to lure his prey by opening up a restaurant for birds—until he realizes that birds are even better as friends." —Provided by publisher. • Identifiers: LCCN 2020005739 | ISBN 9780316483117 (hardcover) • Subjects: CYAC: Alligators—Fiction. | Birds—Fiction. | Friendship—Fiction. • Classification: LCC PZ7.S53743 Chm 2021 | DDC [E]—dc23 • LC record available at https://lccn.loc.gov/2020005739 • ISBN: 978-0-316-48311-7 • PRINTED IN CHINA • APS • 10 9 8 7 6 5 4 3 2 1

CHEZ BOB

by

BOB SHEA

L B

LITTLE, BROWN AND COMPANY

NEW YORK BOSTON

Bob worked very
hard at being lazy.

"Being lazy is making me very hungry,"
said Bob to no one.

"Maybe if I ask nicely, a bird will fly in
my mouth and down into my belly."

"No? But I said please AND thank you!" said Bob.

Lucky grass! I wish I had seeds on me.

Then I'd have all the birds I want.

"I will open a birdseed restaurant on my nose.

Birds will come to eat, but I will eat the birds! I will sell my super-smart idea to other lazy alligators. I will be rich and famous and great."

"I will have diamond teeth and a solid-gold hat!
I will be full of yummy, yummy birds!"

Bob opened Chez Bob the very next day.

"Welcome to Chez Bob, which is a real restaurant and not a trick."

MENU

"Let's see...I will have...the birdseed," said the bird, pointing his wing at the only thing on the menu.

"Good choice!" said Bob.

Bob seasoned his seed with all his favorite spices so his customers would taste extra yummy.

"Delicious!" said the bird. "I will tell all my friends!"

"Oh, then I will not eat you," said Bob.

"What?" said the bird.

"I said, 'So nice to meet you,'" said Bob.

And he couldn't wait to meet the bird's tasty friends.

Soon Chez Bob was the talk of the trees.

Birds flew in from all over the world to eat on Bob's face.

It wasn't long before a little town sprang up around Chez Bob.

The birds built a school, a library, a little park, and an extensive public transportation system.

That's weird since birds can fly, thought Bob.

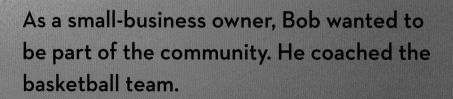

As a small-business owner, Bob wanted to be part of the community. He coached the basketball team.

It's rewarding to be a positive role model for the birds I'm going to eat, thought Bob.

Since he was new in town, Bob joined a book club to meet some like-minded birds. He hit it off with everyone except the orange bird who never let anyone else talk.

How rude, thought Bob. *I'm totally eating him first.*

Bob treated his best customers to a sunset dinner cruise to thank them for their patronage.

If it weren't for these birds I am going to eat, I'd be out of business, thought Bob.

That night the birds stayed up way past their bedtime chirping about the fun they had with Bob all day.

They look so cozy and warm together, thought Bob. Maybe the birds I am going to eat will invite me for a sleepover sometime.

Bob imagined a sad, lonely song in his head as he tried to fall asleep all by himself.

Maybe I should get a cat to snuggle with—or snack on, he thought.

The next morning Bob was excited to see the birds.

"Hey, guys! I went for a walk this morning and picked some pretty flowers for your nests. Oh, and guess what? I think I saw a turtle! Cool, right?"

But before they got to hear more about
the cool turtle, the sky turned dark and...

KEEE-RACK!

"Oh my goodness! A storm!" shouted Bob. "Quick! Everyone fly into my mouth for safety!"

The startled little birds swarmed into Bob's gaping jaws to escape the storm.

Now is my chance to eat the birds,
thought Bob. *I cannot wait to see the looks on their beaks when they check out my diamond teeth and solid-gold hat! They will be jealous and amazed.*

But the little birds would not see Bob's hat or teeth. All the little birds would be inside Bob's belly.

Bob looked around at the quiet, empty town.

A solid-gold hat seemed kind of silly now. Diamond teeth didn't seem so cool anymore.

Bob could hear the birds in his mouth
laughing, playing, and cleaning his teeth.

Bob
knew
what
he
had
to
do.

"Yay! Bob saved us!"

cheered the birds that Bob probably was not going to eat.

"I don't think *hero* is too strong a word, do you?" asked Bob.

"And a hero deserves a super-secret hero surprise!" said a bird who was very excited. "Follow us!"

"We've been working on a Bob-sized nest especially for you!" said a bird who was good at keeping secrets.

"Now we can be together always!" said a bird with a big heart.

"Oh my gosh, you are all so sweet! And I should know, since I just spit you out," said Bob to the birds he was

absolutely,

without a doubt,

definitely *not*

going to eat.